Geronimo Stilton
ENGLISH!

17 WHAT'S YOUR JOB? 你的工作是什麼？

U0061311

新雅文化事業有限公司
www.sunya.com.hk

Geronimo Stilton English
WHAT'S YOUR JOB? 你的工作是什麼?

作　　者：Geronimo Stilton 謝利連摩・史提頓
譯　　者：申倩
責任編輯：王燕參
封面繪圖：Giuseppe Facciotto
插圖繪畫：Claudio Cernuschi, Andrea Denegri, Daria Cerchi
內文設計：Angela Ficarelli, Raffaella Picozzi
出　　版：新雅文化事業有限公司
　　　　　香港筲箕灣耀興道3號東匯廣場9樓
　　　　　營銷部電話：（852）2562 0161
　　　　　客戶服務部電話：（852）2976 6559
　　　　　傳真：（852）2597 4003
　　　　　網址：http://www.sunya.com.hk
　　　　　電郵：marketing@sunya.com.hk
發　　行：香港聯合書刊物流有限公司
　　　　　香港新界大埔汀麗路36號中華商務印刷大廈3字樓
　　　　　電話：（852）2150 2100　傳真：（852）2407 3062
　　　　　電郵：info@suplogistics.com.hk
印　　刷：C & C Offset Printing Co.,Ltd
　　　　　香港新界大埔汀麗路36號
版　　次：二〇一二年一月初版
　　　　　10 9 8 7 6 5 4 3 2 1

CONTENTS
目錄

BENJAMIN'S CLASSMATES
班哲文的老師和同學們

Maestra Topitilla
托比蒂拉・德・托比莉斯

Rarin
拉琳

Diego
迪哥

Rupa
露芭

Tui
杜爾

David
大衛

Sakura
櫻花

Mohamed
穆哈麥德

Tian Kai
田凱

Oliver
奧利佛

Milenko
米蘭哥

Trippo
特里普

Carmen
卡敏

Atina
阿提娜

Esmeralda
愛絲梅拉達

Pandora
潘朵拉

Takeshi
北野

Kuti
菊花

Benjamin
班哲文

Hsing
阿星

Laura
羅拉

Kiku
奇哥

Antonia
安東妮婭

Liza
麗莎

GERONIMO AND HIS FRIENDS
謝利連摩和他的家鼠朋友們

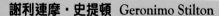

謝利連摩·史提頓 Geronimo Stilton
一個古怪的傢伙，簡直可以說是一隻笨拙的文化鼠。他是
《鼠民公報》的總裁，正花盡心思改變報紙業的歷史。

菲·史提頓 Tea Stilton
謝利連摩的妹妹，她是《鼠民公報》的特派記者，同
時也是一個運動愛好者。

班哲文·史提頓 Benjamin Stilton
謝利連摩的小侄兒，常被叔叔稱作「我的
小乳酪」，是一隻感情豐富的小老鼠。

潘朵拉·華之鼠 Pandora Woz
柏蒂·活力鼠的姨甥女、班哲文最好的朋友，
是一隻活潑開朗的小老鼠。

柏蒂·活力鼠 Patty Spring
美麗迷人的電視新聞工作者，致力於她熱愛的電視事業。

賴皮 Trappola
謝利連摩的表弟，非常喜歡食物，風趣幽默，是一隻饞
嘴、愛開玩笑的老鼠，善於將歡樂傳遞給每一隻鼠。

麗萍姑媽 Zia Lippa
謝利連摩的姑媽，對鼠十分友善，又和藹可親，只想將
最好的給身邊的鼠。

艾拿 Iena
謝利連摩的好朋友，充滿活力，熱愛各項運動，他希望
能把對運動的熱誠傳給謝利連摩。

史奎克·愛管閒事鼠 Ficcanaso Squitt
謝利連摩的好朋友，是一個非常有頭腦的私家
偵探，總是穿着一件黃色的乾濕褸。

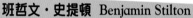
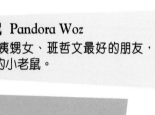

A WALK ROUND THE NEIGHBOURHOOD
在社區裏逛街

親愛的小朋友，你喜歡吃乳酪嗎？我很喜歡呢！我喜歡一點一點地吃乳酪，我喜歡把新鮮乳酪塗在麵包上吃，還喜歡把水牛乳酪弄成粉末吃，更不用說融化的軟軟的乳酪了……我以一千塊莫澤雷勒乳酪發誓，一提起乳酪，我的口水都流出來了！柏蒂今天要留在家裏工作，她託我照顧潘朵拉，於是我打算帶班哲文和潘朵拉去乳酪市場買乳酪。

跟我謝利連摩·史提頓一起學英文，
就像玩遊戲一樣簡單好玩！

你可以一邊看着圖畫一邊讀。
以下有幾個標誌，你要特別留意：

當看到 💿 標誌時，你可以聽CD，
一邊聽，一邊跟着朗讀，還可以跟
着一起唱歌。

當看到 ✪ 標誌時，你可以和朋友
們一起玩遊戲，或者嘗試回答問
題。題目很簡單，它們對鞏固你所
學過的內容很有幫助。

當看到 ❗ 標誌時，你要注意看一
下格子裏的生字，反覆唸幾遍，掌
握發音。

最後，不要忘記完成小測驗和練習
冊裏的問題！看看你有多聰明吧。

祝大家學得開開心心！

謝利連摩·史提頓

LOOK AT ALL THESE SHOPS!
各式各樣的商店

要去乳酪市場，我們要穿過妙鼠城的中心街道，那裏有很多不同的商店。一起來看看這些商店賣什麼，並學習用英語說出這些商店的名稱吧！

What's your job?

BAKERY

I'm a baker. I make bread!

bread

PASTRY SHOP

pastry cook

cakes

tea-cakes

The pastry cook makes cakes.

COFFEE BAR

barman

waiter

waitress

The waiter and the waitress take orders.

CLOCK SHOP

clock

watch

watchmaker

The watchmaker sells and repairs watches and clocks.

CLOTHES SHOP

clothes

shop assistant

The shop assistant sells clothes.

8

BOOKSHOP

books

bookseller

The bookseller sells books.

TOYSHOP

toyman

toys

The toyman sells toys.

FLOWER SHOP

flower seller

flowers

The flower seller sells flowers.

GREENGROCER'S (SHOP)

greengrocer

fruit

vegetables

The greengrocer sells vegetables and fruit.

BUTCHER'S SHOP

butcher

meat

The butcher sells meat.

9

AT THE STATIONER'S
文具店

接着，我們經過一家文具店。我要買一本小筆記簿和一枝原子筆。我以一千塊莫澤雷勒乳酪發誓，文具店裏的貨品真多啊，令鼠眼花繚亂，真的不知道選哪一件才好⋯⋯

STATIONERY

pen

diary

notebook

tape

coloured pencils

 exercise books

ruled exercise book

squared exercise book

pencil case

sketchbook

pencil

glue

 scissors

AT THE ICE CREAM PARLOUR 雪糕店

走出了文具店，這時太陽正高高的掛在天空上，天氣真熱啊！真想吃一杯冰凍的雪糕呢！哦，我記起大街上有一家很出名的雪糕店，我以一千塊莫澤雷勒乳酪發誓，那裏的雪糕好吃極了！

ICE CREAM FLAVOURS
不同口味的雪糕

strawberry　士多啤梨

vanilla　雲呢拿

chocolate　朱古力

hazelnut　榛子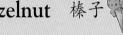

peppermint　薄荷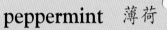

pistachio　開心果

lemon　檸檬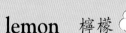

A Fantastic Ice Cream Maker

When I go to the country
I always meet my friend Jack.
He's a special ice cream maker,
he makes fabulous ice cream!
Red strawberry ice cream,
brown chocolate ice cream,
green apple ice cream, ice cream!

We all love ice cream,
it's sweet and coloured!
Jack is a fantastic ice cream maker,
the best in the world!
Orange apricot ice cream,
pink watermelon ice cream,
yellow cheese ice cream!

This ice cream is very good!

Mine is better than yours!

No, my ice cream is the best!

good　好
better　更好
the best　最好

A PETROL STATION 加油站

吃完雪糕後，我們繼續往前走。我看見一輛很熟悉的電單車，我以一千塊莫澤雷勒乳酪發誓，這是菲的車！沒錯，就是她，她正在加油站給她的電單車加油呢。

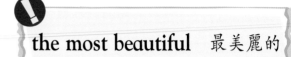

the most beautiful　最美麗的

petrol　汽油
petrol station　加油站
petrol pump　汽油泵
petrol pump attendant　加油員
lead-free petrol　無鉛汽油
diesel fuel　柴油
self service　自助

bucket　水桶
fill up　入滿
pump up the tyres　給輪胎充氣
wash the windows　洗窗子
sponge　海綿
cloth　抹布
car wash　洗車

What are you doing?
你正在做什麼？

AT THE CHEESE MARKET
乳酪市場

我和孩子們終於來到乳酪市場了，這裏有老鼠島上最好的乳酪出售，味道濃郁極了！

cow's milk cheese

goat's milk cheese

sheep's milk cheese

mild cheese

mature cheese

spicy cheese

full-fat cheese

low-fat cheese

grated cheese

Gorgonzola cheese

Mozzarella

cheese spread

cottage cheese

slices of cheese

soft cheese

Stilton cheese is excellent. It's the best!

Mozzarella is softer than mature cheese!

Parmesan cheese

Stilton cheese

⭐ 你喜歡吃乳酪嗎？試着用英語
說出：「我喜歡吃乳酪！」

答案：I like cheese!

THERE ARE LOTS OF JOBS!
各行各業

逛了這麼久，我們要回家了。在回家的路上，我和孩子們都有點累了，所以我們決定走另一條較快捷的路，希望能早點回到家。我們在路上看到另外一些店子，班哲文和潘朵拉很想知道這些店子的英文名稱，以及它們是做什麼的，於是我便向他們一一講解，你也跟着一起學習吧！

NEWSSTAND

newsagent

newspapers

The newsagent sells newspapers.

SHOE SHOP

shoemaker

In a shoe shop you can buy shoes.

shoe repairer

BANK

accountant

teller

In a bank you can change money.

ELECTRICAL APPLIANCES SHOP

electrician

An electrician repairs electrical appliances.

I need to have my moustache trimmed!

BARBER

BARBER

I have just had a haircut!

hairdresser

What's your job?

I'm a hairdresser!

POLICE STATION

policeman
policewoman

The policeman protects citizens.

PHARMACY

pharmacist
medicines

The pharmacist sells medicines.

street sweeper
rubbish container

The street sweeper cleans the streets.

GARAGE

mechanic

The mechanic fixes cars.

POST OFFICE

mail
postman
parcel
letter

The postman delivers the mail.

FIRE STATION

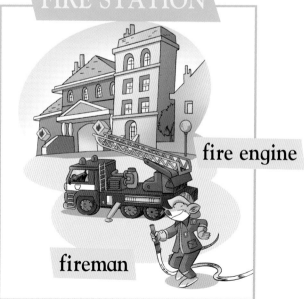

fire engine
fireman

When a fire breaks out, the firemen rush to put it out.

UNDER CONSTRUCTION
工程進行中

快到家的時候，我們經過一個地方，那裏傳出非常嘈吵的聲音，於是我們停下腳步，好奇地窺探一下，裏面有很多鼠正忙着做不同的工作⋯⋯

BUILDING SITE

engineer — architect — land surveyor

bricklayer — painter — workman — carpenter

plumber — gardener

concrete mixer — bulldozer operator — lorry driver

bricks — concrete — wheelbarrow — shovel

 你知道怎樣用英語說出「貨車司機」和「木匠」嗎？說說看。

16

原來這裏是一個建築工地，怪不得有那麼多不同專業的鼠在這裏工作。我們還跟這裏的建築師聊起天來，看看我們問了建築師一些什麼問題。

the latest　最新的

WHAT'S YOUR JOB?
你的工作是什麼？

經過這一天，班哲文和潘朵拉認識了很多不同職業的英文名稱。但是他們總是想學習更多的新知識，於是他們又訪問了他們所認識的鼠的職業是什麼⋯⋯當然是用英語問了，你也跟着一起說說看。

A SONG FOR YOU!

 Track 2

What Will I Be?

On Saturdays I go shopping
with my mother,
I meet the greengrocer
who sells fruit.
Bob the baker bakes bread
and Ralph the milkman
makes tasty cheese
and I wonder...

postman, engineer
dentist, musician
teacher, doctor, journalist or baker
I wonder, I wonder...
what will I be?
I like looking at the shop windows,
the bookseller sells
very interesting books,
Mat the shoemaker repairs a pair of shoes
but Tom the toy maker is my favourite!
And I wonder...

I'm a dentist.

I'm a vet.

I'm a teacher.

I'm a film director.

I'm a cleaning lady.

I'm a librarian.

I'm a delivery man.

I'm a chef.

I'm a journalist.

I'm a detective.

THE ACCIDENTAL COOK

"FROMAGE D'OR" Restaurant. A very special evening.

Good evening, Mr. Saltimbocca.

That's the famous food critic! He's here to rate the food in the restaurant!

Tonight Geronimo Stilton is not here to eat: he has to write an article on Mr. Saltimbocca's dinner.

〈意外當上了廚師〉

這是一個非常特別的晚上，在FROMAGE D'OR餐廳裏……

女侍應：你好，沙添波卡先生。

謝利連摩：那是著名的食評家。他來這家餐廳評價這裏的食物。

這天晚上，謝利連摩不是來這裏吃東西，而是為了寫一篇關於沙添波卡先生吃晚餐的文章。

女侍應：《紅乳酪飲食指南》的沙添波卡先生今天到這裏來了。
廚師：不用驚惶。

謝利連摩：我要寫一篇關於他的晚餐的文章⋯⋯
女侍應：⋯⋯因此今晚每一道菜式都要做到最完美。
廚師：對，請你們現在讓開，我要工作了！

謝利連摩：這味道真香！是什麼味道？
廚師：這是意大利粉，配上四種不同的乳酪醬汁。
謝利連摩：這枝筆怎麼寫不出字來！

謝利連摩：糟了，墨水噴進了鍋子裏。　廚師：史提頓先生，你在做什麼？！？

21

So...

結果……
女侍應：這是墨魚汁意大利粉，希望你喜歡。
沙添波卡：謝謝你！

女侍應：我不想看了。
廚師：現在請讓開！我要準備辣乳酪果批。
謝利連摩：好的，我會靜靜地留在這裏。

廚師：燈關了！我不能做果批了！

女侍應：燭光配炒蛋。
沙添波卡：真是有情調啊！

謝利連摩：沒有果批，只有炒蛋。那麼我要把這頁扔掉。

廚師：你最起碼沒有破壞這個蛋糕，史提頓先生！我要把它放進焗爐了！

謝利連摩：這是用來做蛋糕的麵團，不是廢紙箱嗎？！？

沙添波卡：嗯……這蛋糕裏放的是什麼？　　女侍應、謝利連摩、廚師：我們這次完了！

沙添波卡：太好了！你們竟然把下次光臨的建議菜式藏在蛋糕裏，而且每一道菜都做得這麼美味和獨特。

廚師：史提頓先生，謝謝你！

謝利連摩：呀……不客氣……

TEST 小測驗

⭐ 1. 用英語說出下面的詞彙。

(a) 衣服

(b) 服裝店

(c) 花

(d) 花店

(e) 朱古力雪糕

(f) 士多啤梨雪糕

⭐ 2. 用英語說出班哲文和謝利連摩的對話。

謝利連摩叔叔，
你的工作是什麼？
What's ... ... ,
Uncle Geronimo?

我是一個作家。
I'm ... .

⭐ 3. 用英語說出下面的句子。

(a) 我能幫你嗎？

How can ... ... ?

(b) 我想買一枝鉛筆，麻煩你。

A ... , please.

⭐ 4. 把下面意思相關的字詞用線連起來。

good •   • the most beautiful

beautiful •   • the smallest

small •   • the best

⭐ 5. 用英語回答下面的問題。

(a) Where can you change money? **(b)** Who cleans the streets?

(c) Where can you buy shoes? **(d)** Who delivers the mail?

DICTIONARY 詞典

（英、粵、普發聲）

A

accountant　會計

architect　建築師

B

baker　麵包師傅

bakery　麵包店

barber　理髮師

barman　酒保

bookseller　書店售貨員

bookshop　書店

bread　麵包

bricklayer　泥水匠

building site　建築工地

bulldozer operator

　推土機操控員

butcher　肉販

C

cake　蛋糕

car wash　洗車

carpenter　木匠

chef　廚師

cleaning lady　清潔女工

clock　時鐘

cloth　抹布

clothes　衣服

coffee bar　咖啡館

concrete mixer

　混凝土攪拌機

conductor　指揮家

D

delivery man　速遞員

dentist　牙醫

detective　偵探

diary　日記簿
　　（普：日記本）

diesel fuel　柴油

doctor　醫生

gardener　園丁

glue　膠水

greengrocer　蔬菜水果商

E

electrical appliances　電器

electrician　電器技工

engineer　工程師

H

haircut　剪頭髮

hairdresser　美髮師

hazelnut　榛子

F

fill up　入滿

film director　導演

fire engine　消防車

fire station　消防局

fireman　消防員

flowers　花

fruit　水果

J

job　工作

journalist　記者

judge　法官

L

land surveyor　土地測量師

lawyer　律師

lemon　檸檬

letter　信件

librarian　圖書館管理員

lorry driver　貨車司機

G

garage　汽車修理廠

M

mail　郵件

meat　肉

mechanic　汽車修理技工

medicines　藥

motorbike　電單車
　　（普：摩托車）

musician　音樂家

N

newsagent　報紙經銷商

newspaper　報紙

newsstand　報攤

notary　公證人

notebook　筆記簿

nurse　護士

P

painter　油漆工人

parcel　包裹

pastry cook　點心師傅

peppermint　薄荷

petrol　汽油

petrol pump　汽油泵

petrol pump attendant
　　加油員

petrol station　加油站

pharmacist　藥劑師

pharmacy　藥房

photographer　攝影師

pianist　鋼琴家

pistachio　開心果

plumber　水喉技工

police station　警署

policeman　警員

policewoman　女警

postman　郵差

R

rubbish container　垃圾桶

ruled exercise book
　　印有橫行的練習簿

S

scissors 剪刀

self service 自助

shoe repairer 補鞋匠

shoemaker 鞋匠

shop assistant 店員

shovel 鏟子

singer 歌手

sketchbook 畫簿

sponge 海綿

squared exercise book
  印有格子的練習簿

stationery 文具

strawberry 士多啤梨
  （普：草莓）

street sweeper 清道夫

T

tape 膠紙

taxi driver 的士司機

teacher 老師

teller 出納員

toyman 玩具商人

V

vanilla 雲呢拿（普：香草）

vegetables 蔬菜

vet 獸醫

W

waiter 侍應（普：服務員）

waitress 女侍應
  （普：女服務員）

watch 手錶

watchmaker 鐘錶匠

watermelon 西瓜

wheelbarrow 獨輪小車

workman 工人

writer 作家

看在一千塊莫澤雷勒乳酪的份上，你學得開心嗎？很開心，對不對？好極了！跟你一起跳舞唱歌我也很開心！我等着你下次繼續跟班哲文和潘朵拉一起玩一起學英語呀。現在要說再見了，當然是用英語說啦！

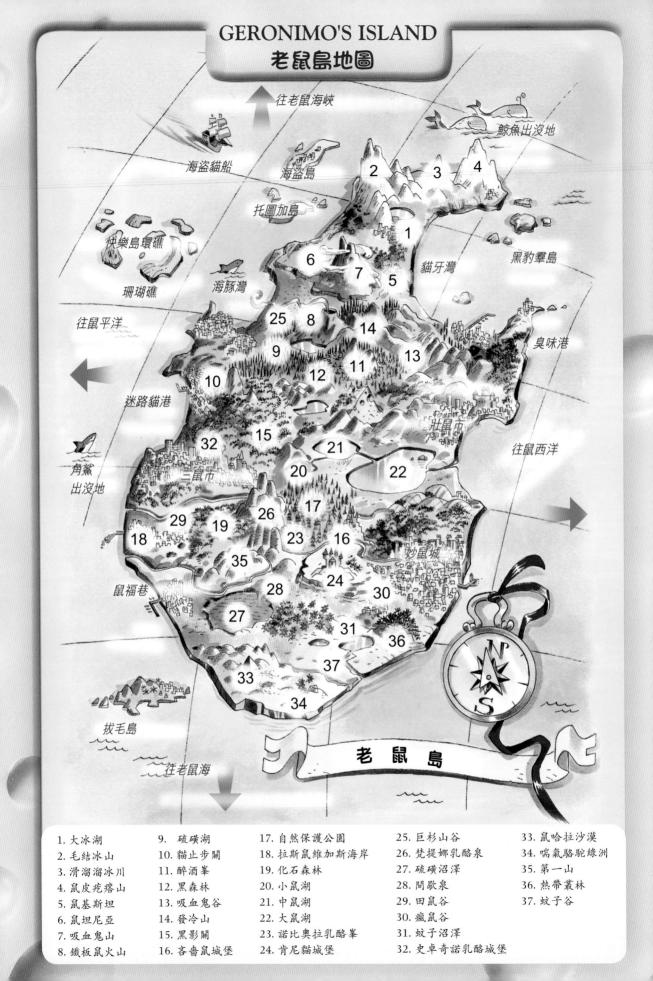

GERONIMO'S ISLAND
老鼠島地圖

往老鼠海峽

鯨魚出沒地

海盜貓船

海盜島

托圖加島

黑豹羣島

快樂島環礁

珊瑚礁

海豚灣

貓牙灣

臭味港

往鼠平洋

迷路貓港

壯鼠市

往鼠西洋

角鯊
出沒地

三鼠市

妙鼠城

鼠福巷

拔毛島

往老鼠海

老鼠島

Geronimo Stilton

EXERCISE BOOK

練習冊

想知道自己對 WHAT'S YOUR JOB? 掌握了多少，
趕快打開後面的練習完成它吧！

ENGLISH!

17 **WHAT'S YOUR JOB?** 你的工作是什麼？

THERE ARE LOTS OF JOBS!
各行各業

⭐ 看看下面的圖畫，他們的職業是什麼？把代表答案的英文字母寫在句框裏。

A. I'm a taxi driver.　　B. I'm a detective.
C. I'm a vet.　　　　　　D. I'm a nurse.
E. I'm a film director.

WHAT'S YOUR JOB?
你的工作是什麼？

⭐ 1. 看看下面的圖畫，他們的工作是什麼？根據提示，選出正確的詞彙填在橫線上，完成句子。

提示：flowers
seller
sells
greengrocer
fruit
shop

(a)

The

_____

assistant

_____

clothes.

(b)

The flower

_____

sells

_____.

The

_____

sells vegetables and

_____.

(c)

★ 2. 把不同的職業和與它相關的工作用線連起來。

The butcher •   • repairs watches and clocks.

The baker •   • makes bread.

The pastry cook •   • sells books.

The waiter •   • makes cakes.

The toyman •   • sells meat.

The bookseller •   • sells toys.

The watchmaker •   • takes orders.

AT THE STATIONER'S
文具店

⭐ 文具店裏售賣很多不同的文具，你知道這些文具的英文名稱嗎？根據提示，選出正確的詞彙填在橫線上。

提示：pen
pencil case
notebook
scissors
glue
tape

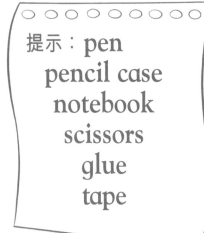

1. _____

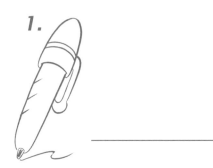

2. _____

3. _____

4. _____

5. _____

6. _____

HOW CAN I HELP YOU?
我能幫你嗎？

⭐ 1. 看看下面的圖畫，根據提示，選出正確的詞彙填在橫線上，
完成句子。

How can I help you?

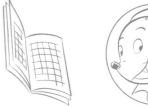

(a) The biggest _____ exercise book you have, please!

提示：

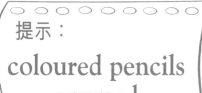

coloured pencils
squared
sketchbook

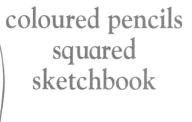

(b) A box of _____

and a _____ .

⭐ 2. 根據指示，把正確的圖畫圈起來。

(a) The biggest exercise book

(b) The smallest box of coloured pencils

AT THE ICE CREAM PARLOUR 雪糕店

⭐ 謝利連摩和潘朵拉買了各種不同口味的雪糕，你知道有哪些口味嗎？在橫線上寫出缺少的英文字母，然後給圖畫填上適當的顏色。

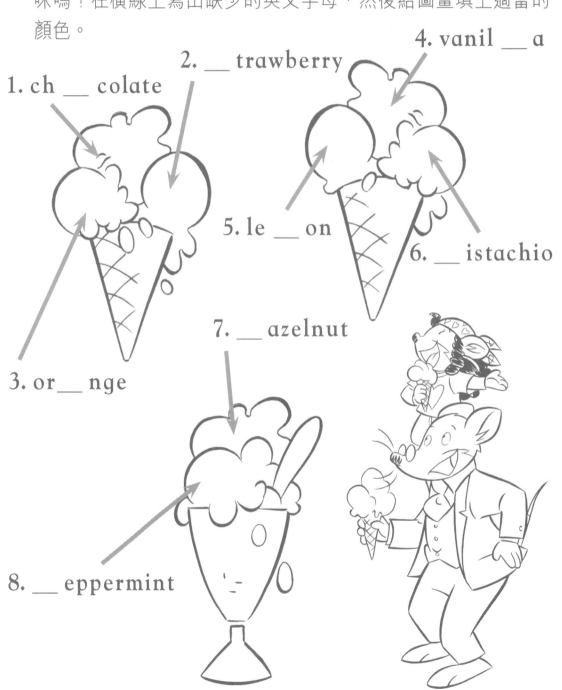

1. ch __ colate

2. __ trawberry

3. or __ nge

4. vanil __ a

5. le __ on

6. __ istachio

7. __ azelnut

8. __ eppermint

UNDER CONSTRUCTION
工程進行中

★ 在建築工地上你會看見些什麼？根據圖畫，選出正確的詞彙填在橫線上。

> plumber   shovel   gardener   bricklayer
> bricks   carpenter   painter

1. _____

2. _____

3. _____

4. _____

6. _____

5. _____

7. _____

7

ANSWERS 答案

TEST 小測驗

1. (a) clothes   (b) clothes shop   (c) flower / flowers   (d) flower shop
   (e) chocolate ice cream   (f) strawberry ice cream
2. Benjamin: What's <u>your job</u>, Uncle Geronimo?   Geronimo: I'm <u>a writer</u>.
3. (a) How can <u>I help you</u>?   (b) A <u>pencil</u>, <u>please</u>.
4. good ●   ● the most beautiful
   beautiful ●   ● the smallest
   small ●   ● the best
5. (a) in a bank   (b) the street sweeper   (c) in a shoe shop   (d) the postman

EXERCISE BOOK 練習冊

P.1

1. D   2. E   3. A   4. C   5. B

P.2-3

1. (a) shop, sells   b) seller, flowers   (c) greengrocer, fruit

2. The butcher ●   ● repairs watches and clocks.
   The baker ●   ● makes bread.
   The pastry cook ●   ● sells books.
   The waiter ●   ● makes cakes.
   The toyman ●   ● sells meat.
   The bookseller ●   ● sells toys.
   The watchmaker ●   ● takes orders.

P.4

1. pen   2. glue   3. notebook   4. scissors   5. tape   6. pencil case

P.5

1. (a) squared   (b) coloured pencils, sketchbook

2. (a) 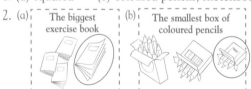 The biggest exercise book   (b) The smallest box of coloured pencils

P.6

1. ch<u>o</u>colate   2. <u>s</u>trawberry   3. or<u>a</u>nge   4. vani<u>ll</u>a
5. le<u>m</u>on   6. <u>p</u>istachio   7. <u>h</u>azelnut   8. <u>p</u>eppermint

P.7

1. shovel   2. bricks   3. bricklayer   4. carpenter   5. painter   6. plumber   7. gardener